THIS WALKER BOOK BELONGS TO:

_____

_____

_____

_____

This book has been assessed as Stage 8
according to *Individualised Reading*, by
Bernice and Cliff Moon, published by
The Centre for the Teaching of Reading,
University of Reading
School of Education.

First published 1986 by Walker Books Ltd
87 Vauxhall Walk, London SE11 5HJ

This edition published 1989

Printed in Italy by Lito di Roberto Terrazzi

British Library Cataloguing in Publication Data
King-Smith, Dick
H. Prince.
I. Title II. Honeysett, Martin
823'.914[J] PZ7
ISBN 0-7445-1357-X

H. PRINCE

written by Dick King~Smith

illustrated by Martin Honeysett

WALKER BOOKS
LONDON

There was once a frog named H. Prince.
He lived in a dirty duck pond
with his mother, Mrs Prince,
and his father, Mr Prince.

H. Prince often wondered
what the H stood for.

Was he Henry? Was he Herbert?

Was he Humphrey?

'What does H stand for?'
he asked his mother one day.

But she only answered, 'Hop it!'

He went to look for his father.

'What does H stand for?' he asked.

But his father only said, 'Hop it!'

H. Prince was not very happy about this.

He blinked his eyes and

his mouth turned down at the corners.

But then he made up his mind.

He had to know what H stood for.

So he decided to leave home and find out.

He hopped out of the duck pond and
found himself in a field.

He hopped out of the field and
found himself by a road.

H. Prince hopped off down the road.

Soon he met a cat strolling along the road.

'Excuse me,' said H. Prince politely.

'What does H stand for?'

'Hop it!' said the cat, and

 hissed at the frog.

Next he met a dog trotting along the road.

'Excuse me,' said H. Prince politely.

'What does H stand for?'

'Hop it!' said the dog, and
growled at the frog.

Then he met a girl on a bike

pedalling along the road.

'Excuse me,' said H. Prince politely once again.

'What does H stand for?'

'Hop it!' said the girl on the bike,

and rang her bell at the frog.

Last of all he met a man driving a big lorry.
It was going fast and
before H. Prince could open his mouth,
the man sounded the horn and
shouted at the frog.
'HOP IT!' he bellowed
at the top of his voice.

H. Prince hopped it, just in time.

He was not very happy about this.

He blinked his eyes and

his mouth turned down at the corners.

Sadly he hopped off the road and
found himself in a garden.
He hopped down the garden and
found himself by a goldfish pool.
It was not a bit like the dirty duck pond.
It was a beautiful goldfish pool,
covered in beautiful water-lilies.
On one of the water-lilies
sat a beautiful frog.

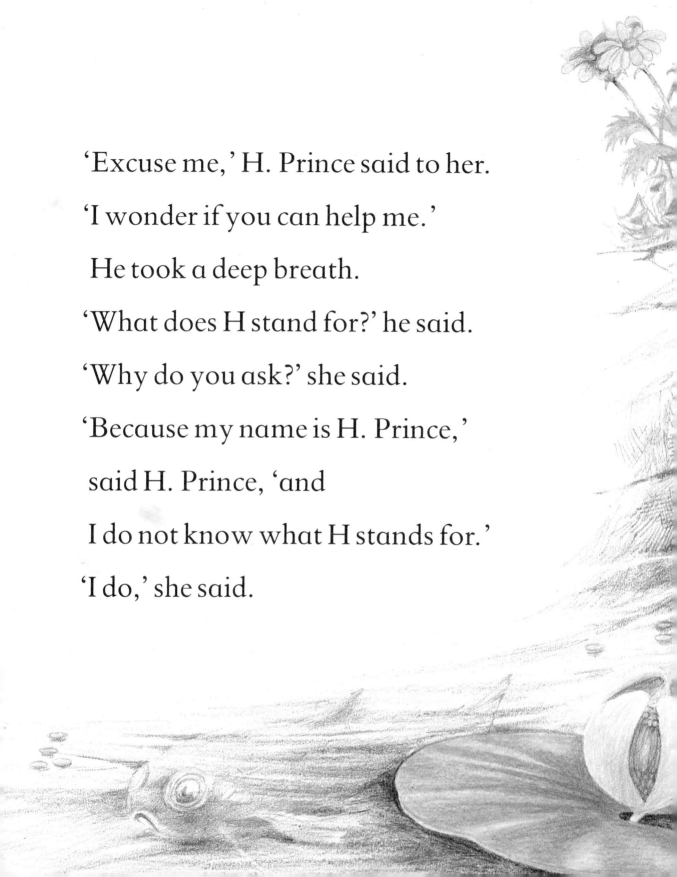

'Excuse me,' H. Prince said to her.

'I wonder if you can help me.'

He took a deep breath.

'What does H stand for?' he said.

'Why do you ask?' she said.

'Because my name is H. Prince,'

said H. Prince, 'and

I do not know what H stands for.'

'I do,' she said.

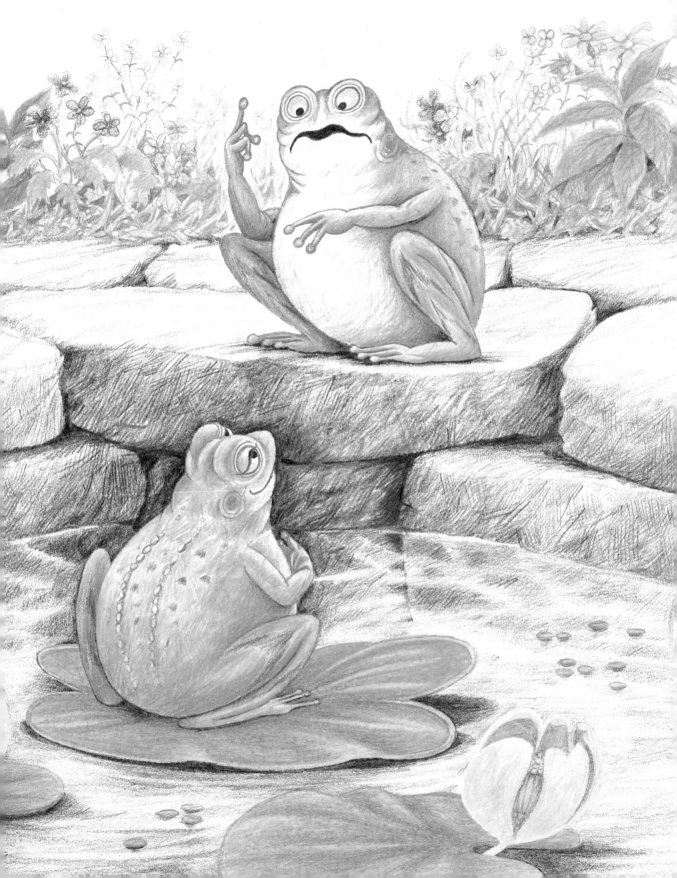

H. Prince blinked his eyes and

his mouth turned down at the corners.

I know what she will say, he thought sadly.

She will say what Mother and Father said.

She will say what the cat and

the dog and the girl on the bike and

the man in the lorry said.

She will say 'Hop it!'

He waited but the frog did not speak.

She only gazed at him

with her beautiful bulgy eyes.

H. Prince took another deep breath.

'What does H stand for?' he said.

'H,' said the beautiful frog,

'stands for Handsome.'

H. Prince was very happy about this.

His eyes shone and

his mouth turned up at the corners.

'Yes,' she said,

'you are my very own Handsome Prince.

Hop in!' So H. Prince hopped in, and

they lived happily ever after.

MORE WALKER PAPERBACKS

THE PRE-SCHOOL YEARS

John Satchwell
& Katy Sleight
Monster Maths
ODD ONE OUT   BIG AND LITTLE
COUNTING   SHAPES   ADD ONE   SORTING
WHAT TIME IS IT?   TAKE AWAY ONE

FOR THE VERY YOUNG

John Burningham
Concept books
COLOURS   ALPHABET
OPPOSITES   NUMBERS

Byron Barton
TRAINS   TRUCKS   BOATS   AEROPLANES

PICTURE BOOKS
For All Ages

Colin McNaughton
THERE'S AN AWFUL LOT OF WEIRDOS IN
OUR NEIGHBOURHOOD
SANTA CLAUS IS SUPERMAN

Russell Hoban
& Colin McNaughton
The Hungry Three
THEY CAME FROM AARGH!
THE GREAT FRUIT GUM ROBBERY

Jill Murphy
FIVE MINUTES' PEACE
ALL IN ONE PIECE

Bob Graham
THE RED WOOLLEN BLANKET
HAS ANYONE HERE SEEN WILLIAM?

Philippa Pearce
& John Lawrence
EMILY'S OWN ELEPHANT

David Lloyd
& Charlotte Voake
THE RIDICULOUS STORY OF
GAMMER GURTON'S NEEDLE

Nicola Bayley
Copycats
SPIDER CAT   PARROT CAT   CRAB CAT
POLAR BEAR CAT   ELEPHANT CAT

Peter Dallas-Smith
& Peter Cross
TROUBLE FOR TRUMPETS

Philippe Dupasquier
THE GREAT ESCAPE

Sally Scott
THE THREE WONDERFUL BEGGARS

Bamber Gascoigne
& Joseph Wright
AMAZING FACTS BOOKS 1 & 2

Martin Handford
WHERE'S WALLY?
WHERE'S WALLY NOW?